Weekly Reader Books

THE GHOSTS AT MANOR HOUSE

WEEKLY READER BOOKS PRESENTS

THE GHOSTS AT MANOR HOUSE

By G. C. Skipper

Illustrated by Dick Smolinski

CHILDRENS PRESS · CHICAGO

Library of Congress Cataloging in Publication Data

Skipper, G   C
    The ghosts at Manor House

    SUMMARY: While doing research for their term
paper, two youngsters find it difficult to ignore
rumors about the ghosts haunting the site of a
colonial ironworks.
    [1. Ghost stories] I. Smolinsksi, Dick.
II. Title.
PZ7.S62817Gh   [Fic]   77-17270
ISBN 0-516-03472-3

For my wife, Ann . . .
who has never failed
to love and believe

THE
GHOSTS
AT MANOR
HOUSE

Just as Charles Sawyer's father hurried through the front door, the telephone on the table at the bottom of the stairs shrilled urgently.

"I'll get it!" Charles yelled and clumped down the stairs two at a time.

"Go slow, mister," his father warned. Charles reached the bottom and whirled around the bannister toward the phone. "Yes, sir," he said. The phone rang again.

"Noisy as a cage of parrots," Charles heard his father say. As he picked up the phone, Charles looked over his shoulder, grinning. His father always made jokes about the noisy household.

Charles's father opened the hall closet to hang up his coat. When he swung the door open he gave a yelp as Post Toasties, the cat, streaked out of the closet. The cat slipped and skidded across the polished floor and turned a corner, all claws and clatter.

"Who shut the cat in the closet?" Mr. Sawyer asked in a loud voice.

"Is that you, dear?" Mrs. Sawyer called from the kitchen.

"Right now I'm not sure," came the reply.

Charles had spoken into the telephone. "Hello?"

"What on earth is going on over there? I've never heard so much noise in my life!"

"Oh, hi, Carol," Charles said. "Everything's happening at the same time. Dad just came in from work and Post Toasties was closed up in the closet and the phone was ringing."

"Maybe I should call back later," Carol said. On the phone her voice sounded much older than her fourteen years. Charles wondered if he still sounded like a kid to her. After all, she was only a few months older than he. Deliberately he lowered his voice. "No, it's all right. What's up?"

"I think I've forgotten why I called," Carol laughed. "You're sure I'm not adding to the confusion?"

"Of course not," Charles said. "Did you find out anything?"

"I think so. At least I think it's a good idea."

"Anything would be good right now," Charles told her. "I've strained my brain and still can't come up with anything for that term paper—except what everybody else is writing about."

"It has to have historical significance, right?" Carol asked.

"That's right."

"Then why don't we do the paper on Manor House?"

"Manor House! That's nothing but a big museum, isn't it?"

"With fifty-one rooms to be exact," Carol said. "But listen to this." Excitement crept into her voice. "Back before the War of Independence, Manor House was a major ironworks. Pretty important, too. We can trace its history from the war until now."

"It doesn't sound very exciting," Charles said.

"Are you kidding? You know that graveyard near the place?"

"That big, spooky one down the road from the main house?"

"Right! Did you know it's filled with soldiers? They all died of some sort of epidemic. We could work that in and really make something good out of this."

"It's worth a try."

"But listen to the best idea of all," Carol said. "We don't have to depend on library books to get the information. Dad knows the superintendent up there. We could go up some night after the museum closes and interview him and the care-taker. We'll get everything firsthand and use the library to check the dates."

"Like reporters, huh?" Charles said. Carol did not reply. There was a small silence. Then Charles said, "Okay, you talked me into it. Anyway, I want to see that graveyard at night. No telling what's going on up there," he laughed.

"Talk to you later, Charles," Carol said. Her mind was obviously on the term paper and not on ghosts.

As Charles returned the phone to its cradle, his mother came in from the kitchen. She was a tall, pretty woman with short, black hair. She wore jeans and a sweater. "Who was that?" she asked.

"Just Carol. We're doing our term paper on Manor House."

Suddenly his mother's expression changed. It was so fast Charles really didn't know if he'd seen the change or not. Maybe he'd just imagined it. "Anything wrong, Mom?" he asked.

His mother shook her head quickly. "No, I'm sure Manor House will make a good subject. You'd better clean up for dinner."

"Be right down," Charles said.

As he hurried upstairs he couldn't shake the feeling that something had upset his mother, but he didn't know what. Maybe he had imagined it, Charles thought, but for a second she had looked afraid.

CHAPTER 2

Unlike the adventure-filled house where Charles Sawyer lived, Carol Marshall's home was always quiet and orderly. It was a large, rambling place with huge wooden doors, carpeting that silenced the footsteps, and a big library with row after row of leather-bound books. The Marshall home was kept spotless by the housekeeper, Mrs. Barker. Carol's mother had died when Carol was three years old and since then she and her father had lived alone in the house.

Carol's father was a tall, scholarly man with thick white hair and a neat, white moustache. He spent much of his time in the library reading or working.

When Carol entered the study, her father immediately put down his book, placing it on a table near his chair. "Come in," he said. "Mrs. Barker tells me you and Charles are doing research on Manor House. It's quite an interesting place, you know."

Carol hurried to his chair and kissed him on the cheek. He smelled of clean soap and a delicate after shave that always pleased her. She loved her father very much.

"We haven't really done any research yet," she said. Her hair hung in a straight, soft fall below her shoulders. It was the color of maple leaves in autumn. "That's what I wanted to talk to you about."

"You know you're welcome to use anything in the study that can help you."

"I want to do more than that," Carol said. "All the other kids at school will go to musty old books, as usual, and dig out whatever they need and rewrite it. Charles and I want to do something original."

"I like that idea, but Manor House is hardly original," he said. "Hundreds of people visit there every week."

"But we want to talk to the superintendent and

the caretaker and get its history from them. Then we can check dates and all from your books. Could you talk to Mr. Benson?"

"I suppose so," her father said, but there was something reluctant in his voice. "Mrs. Barker doesn't like the idea at all, you know," he said after a while.

"Why not?" Carol asked, surprised and a little angry. She didn't know Mrs. Barker even knew of the term paper. "Why would it matter to her?" Carol asked.

"Young lady," her father said in a stern voice. "Mrs. Barker loves you just as much as I do. She's just concerned."

"I didn't mean to be rude," Carol apologized, "but why is she so concerned about a term paper on Manor House?"

"Didn't you know the place has a rather strange and tragic history?"

"Oh, wow! Really?" Carol flopped down on her knees near her father's chair. This was her favorite position. "What happened? I thought it was only an ironworks."

"Oh, yes, it was an ironworks," her father agreed. "But there are also stories about locked doors that are found opened the next day, and in 1778 there apparently was a holdup. There were also several mining disasters. All kinds of strange things have supposedly happened, and people like Mrs. Barker are still frightened of Manor House. She thinks you shouldn't go up there."

"That would be great material to include in the paper," Carol said.

"I didn't mean to fill your mind with silly stories," Carol's father told her. "I just wanted you to understand how Mrs. Barker feels. Personally, I think the stories are all bunk."

"If we promise to be very, very careful, will you talk to the superintendent?"

Her father smiled. "Yes, of course. I'm sure it will be all right. When would you like to go?"

"Tuesday night, if that's okay with Mr. Benson."

"We'll see," her father said. He gently touched her cheek. "You're very much like your mother, you know."

"I wish I had known her," Carol said.

"She was a lady and she was beautiful and I loved her. I hope you don't mind that I've never married again."

"Oh, Dad," Carol said suddenly. She threw her arms around his neck and hugged him tightly. "I wouldn't want to live anywhere else with anyone else."

There was a soft rap at the door. As Carol stood up, her father said, "Come in, Mrs. Barker."

The housekeeper stood for a moment in the doorway. She held a silver tray on which there was a matching teapot. "I thought you might like some tea," she said.

"Yes, thank you. Over here will be fine," Carol's father said. "We were just discussing Manor House."

Mrs. Barker glanced quickly at Carol as she placed the tray on the table near the chair. "That's a bad place," she said. "All them soldiers dying of a disease, and there's worse things going on up there. Things folks don't understand."

"I told Carol you didn't think she and Charles should go, but now that we've discussed it, I'm sure everything will be fine."

"Of course we'll be okay, Mrs. Barker. But it's sweet of you to worry."

Mrs. Barker, who looked like a tiny stuffed doll in her apron, straightened quickly and shook her

head. "It's none of my business, of course, but I just don't think it's right."

"We'll be fine, Mrs. Barker. We won't be up there late. If it will make you feel better you can come with us."

A look of sheer panic crossed the housekeeper's face. "No, ma'am," she said. "No, ma'am. I'll do my worrying from right here in this house. If your father says it's okay, I'll not say another word." She hurried out of the room.

Carol and her father exchanged glances. Then they laughed despite themselves. "You certainly know how to handle her," Carol's father said.

"I'll tell Charles we'll go Tuesday night," Carol said. She gave her father a quick kiss and ran from the room. Her father watched her leave, then poured himself a cup of hot tea. When Carol had gone, he said aloud, "I just hope those stories are as silly as they seem."

CHAPTER 3

"They're closed!" Mr. Sawyer said. He stopped the car. Ahead of them, lit by the headlights, Charles and Carol could see the iron chain draped across the driveway. A small sign saying "Closed" hung from the chain. The sign flapped in the wind. Beyond the chain a walkway led toward the wide front steps of Manor House.

"It's okay, Mr. Sawyer," Carol said. "Dad said it would probably be closed when we arrived. But the superintendent is expecting us."

"I don't like dropping you kids off like this. It's pretty dark up there, and the rain could start any minute."

"Someone is meeting us," Charles said. "We'll do the interview and Carol's father will be here to take us home by nine."

Mr. Sawyer looked doubtful. "I don't know," he said. "Are you sure you're expected tonight?"

"Yes, sir," Carol answered.

Suddenly Mr. Sawyer laughed. "Listen to me, will you! Every time it threatens to rain I get jumpy."

"That's the way Mrs. Barker is," Carol laughed. Then she added, "But everything's arranged and we'll be all right."

"Tell you what," Mr. Sawyer said. "I'll wait here in the car until you get to the front steps. The headlights will help you see your way."

Charles opened the door and Carol followed, carrying a notebook.

The headlights of the car lighted the walkway in a yellow glow. In a short time they reached the front steps. Charles turned and waved. They stood on the steps and watched Mr. Sawyer back up the car. Then it disappeared down the street, its red tail lights glowing in the dark.

"Sure is quiet," Charles said when the car was gone.

"It sure is," Carol agreed. "I guess we'd better go up."

They started up the stairs, Carol leading the

way. At the porch she stopped suddenly. "Look over there." Carol pointed toward the side of the museum. In the distance there was a wide stretch of open land.

"Looks like a field to me," Charles said.

"Look closely," Carol told him.

At that moment lightning flickered against the horizon. In the momentary glare the open land suddenly appeared bright and clear. They could see row after row of tombstones.

"That's the graveyard!" Charles said.

"Where the soldiers are buried," Carol added.

A clap of thunder followed the lightning and Charles jumped, startled by the sound. Carol laughed, reaching out and grasping his arm.

"What's the matter? Scared?" she teased.

"Of course not," Charles answered. "I just didn't expect the thunder, that's all."

"Well, we're not getting anything done standing out here," Carol said.

They were halfway to the front door when Charles stopped her. He spoke in a low, urgent whisper. "Did you see that?"

"See what?" Carol looked at him, but Charles was staring toward the graveyard.

"That light. There was a light out there."

"Why would anybody be out there at this time of night?" Carol asked. She looked at the graveyard, then back at Charles. "Are you trying to scare me?"

"No, look. Over to the right."

"I don't see anything," Carol said.

"Right there!" Charles cried.

As Carol watched, she suddenly saw the light. It appeared near the edge of the graveyard. "It looks like an old-fashioned lantern," she said. As they watched, the light moved. It seemed to make a small semicircle, then it was still again.

"I wonder who it is," Charles said.

Again the sudden flash of lightning illuminated the entire area. In the harsh glow they saw a man sitting on one of the tombstones. He was holding a lantern.

"He must be crazy!" Charles cried. "What's he doing out there?"

This time the thunder was a low grumble high in the sky. Darkness closed around them again, but still they could see the lantern. As they watched, the light moved abruptly, as if the man had jumped down from the tombstone. Then it

moved across the graveyard, toward the opposite side. They could see the flat, gray tombstones as the light from the lantern touched them. The light moved on in a straight line across the cemetery.

"We'd better go inside," Carol said.

She turned and rapped loudly on the huge front door of the museum. There was no answer. All they heard was the echo of the knocks.

"Here, let me try," Charles said. He beat loudly on the front door.

"Hush, you'll wake the dead," Carol said.

"Very funny," Charles answered. He knocked again, more loudly.

"I didn't mean that," Carol said. "I wasn't trying to be funny."

Almost instinctively, both of them looked toward the graveyard. It was totally dark now. The light had disappeared. Charles turned to knock again. Just as he lifted his fist, the huge front door swung open. The glare of the inside light hit them full in the face. For a moment Carol and Charles were both startled. Then a man said, "Is that you, Carol?"

"Hello, Mr. Benson. Are we on time?"

"Yes, yes," the man said. "Come on in." He swung the door open wider and they entered. Charles felt much more comfortable inside. Mr. Benson, his bald head catching the overhead light in a shiny blur, smiled warmly at them. He shook hands with Carol. "You're certainly growing up, young lady."

"I'd like you to meet Charles Sawyer, Mr. Benson," Carol said. "We're doing the term paper together."

"Very nice to see you," Mr. Benson said with a smile. He shook hands with Charles. "I was afraid the rain would catch you before you arrived."

"We were lucky," Charles said. "It hasn't started yet."

They followed Mr. Benson down a long corridor. Halfway down they reached a door with the word "Office" printed on the dark wood in gold letters.

"We can talk in here," Mr. Benson said. He opened the door and showed Charles and Carol in. "The rest of the building gets a bit drafty at night."

"We certainly appreciate your taking time to talk with us," Carol said.

"My pleasure." Mr. Benson showed them two chairs and asked them to be seated. He sat down behind the desk and asked, "Where would you like to start?"

"Excuse me," Charles said, "but before we get started, we'd also like to talk with the caretaker, if it's okay. That way we can get everything done tonight."

"Certainly," Mr. Benson said. "He's upstairs, I believe. But I warn you, he's a strange man. Nevertheless, I'm sure he'll be pleased."

"He certainly is peculiar," Carol said. She and Charles looked at each other and laughed.

"What do you mean?" Mr. Benson asked, puzzled and frowning.

"We saw him a little while ago," Carol explained.

"Really? Where?" There was an odd expression on Mr. Benson's face.

"Out in the graveyard," Charles said. "He scared us to death with that lantern. I guess he was making the rounds."

Mr. Benson looked at Charles, then turned his gaze toward Carol. "Yes," he said after a moment. "I suppose he was." But Mr. Benson's voice was not convincing.

Before either of them could say anything further, Mr. Benson launched into the history of Manor House. He told how the land had been purchased originally by a family in Newark, New Jersey. They had built the first iron-smelting furnaces on it. "It was a major center at one time, you know," Mr. Benson said proudly. Carol and Charles took notes rapidly. Mr. Benson talked on and on, going into detail about how the house was deeded to the State of New Jersey in 1936 and how it eventually became a museum.

"There you are," the superintendent said after a while. "Is there anything else you'd like to know?" Charles and Carol glanced at each other. They could have gotten this information from the library, they realized.

Carol said after a moment, "Could you tell us about the death of the soldiers who are buried in the graveyard. They were French, weren't they?"

"Yes, they were French, but there's nothing much to tell. It happened during the War of Independence or sometime around that period. Some sort of epidemic. It was a common thing back then."

"And the mining disasters?" Carol asked.

Mr. Benson coughed suddenly and smiled. He

looked very uncomfortable. "I suppose you've heard all those stories again, about this place being haunted, I mean."

"Sir?" Charles asked.

"Oh, sure," Carol added quickly. She nudged Charles rapidly with her knee. "Of course, but this is the kind of added information we'll need. We do want to stick to facts, however."

Mr. Benson straightened some papers on his desk.

"Wait a minute," Charles said. "I haven't heard the stories."

"Old wives' tales, I assure you," Mr. Benson said hastily. "Nothing worth discussing. Now if you'll—"

But before he could finish speaking, they heard footsteps. It sounded as if two people were hurrying down the corridor outside. All of them looked up. Charles and Carol turned and stared toward the door. The footsteps grew louder and louder until they reached the door. Then they stopped abruptly.

"Now who on earth could that be?" Mr. Benson asked under his breath. He got up from behind the desk and hurried to the door. He waited a moment, but when there was no knock, he opened it quickly. He stuck his head out into the corridor. He looked one way, then the other. After a moment he closed the door and returned to the desk. "That's funny," he remarked. "No one was there."

Carol and Charles exchanged glances. "It was probably the caretaker," Charles said.

"Yes," said Mr. Benson, "it must have been." The superintendent moved his chair back without warning. "Well, I think that covers it. Nice of you to drop by."

Carol and Charles looked at him, surprised.

"Thank you," Charles said softly.

"Mr. Benson," Carol said suddenly. She sounded determined and the tone of her voice surprised Charles as well as the superintendent. "We're not quite finished. We'd still like to talk to the caretaker."

"Do you really think it's necessary to interview Ted?"

"Yes, sir," Charles said rapidly.

Mr. Benson glanced at one, then the other. "Very well, then. I'll get him."

"Oh, don't bother," Carol said quickly. She

stood up. "Come on, Charles, we can find him. Besides, I want to see the museum."

Hesitantly, Charles followed Carol toward the door. "Is it okay?" he asked.

"Of course it is," Mr. Benson said, but he was frowning. "Ted's room is on the other side, straight down the corridor at the back. If he's not there I suggest you come back another time."

"We will," Carol said. "And thank you again."

"You're quite welcome," he said, but he was still frowning.

Before Mr. Benson could say anything more Charles and Carol were out in the corridor. They quickly closed the door behind them.

CHAPTER 4

Charles and Carol were deep into the museum. They walked silently, rounded a corner, and went down a long corridor. "I'd hate to get lost in this place," said Charles. He spoke in hushed tones.

"Did Mr. Benson say the caretaker's room was at the end of the corridor?" Carol asked.

"I think so," Charles replied. They were very conscious of the quietness around them. They no longer could see the light from the office. The corridor was dim and shadowy. Ahead of them they saw a large, wide stairway that swept upward. It seemed to disappear in the upper darkness.

"Wait a minute; there he is," Carol said suddenly. She touched Charles's arm and pointed

her notebook toward the stairs. A man moved quickly up the stairs, then just as suddenly was gone.

"Sir! Wait a minute!" Charles called. They both walked quickly forward, but by the time they reached the bottom of the stairs, the figure was gone.

"I wonder why he didn't stop. Surely he heard us," Carol said.

"Mr. Benson said he was a strange man," Charles reminded her.

Suddenly they both shivered. A chill seemed to envelop the bottom of the stairs. "He was right about its being drafty in here. I'm freezing to death," said Carol.

Charles pulled his denim jacket tighter around him. "It wasn't this cold when we came in."

"I suppose we'd better go on up and find the caretaker," Carol said. She shivered in the coldness, then moved quickly up the stairs. Charles was behind her.

"Maybe we shouldn't," he told her. "It's pretty dark up there."

"He has to have a light on. We probably just can't see it from here."

They had walked only a short distance up the stairs when they heard the footsteps again. They came from behind them, from down the corridor where they'd just been. Immediately Charles and Carol froze on the stairs. They looked back down the stairs, waiting. The footsteps were fast, as if two people were hurrying somewhere. They grew louder and louder. Charles and Carol waited, watching the end of the corridor. The footsteps quickened; the people seemed to be nearly running down the corridor.

"Do you think anything's wrong?" Charles asked in a whisper.

"I don't know," Carol said, "but we'll find out soon."

They waited, staring at the end of the corridor. The sound of the footsteps seemed to come closer and closer. Then suddenly it was quiet. There was only a long, lingering silence. All they could hear was their own breathing.

"I don't like this," Charles said. "Somebody else is in here. We're not alone."

Carol swallowed hard. She did not trust her voice to answer. Instead, she took Charles's hand and they continued up the stairs.

They had nearly reached the point where the deep shadow fell across the stairs when suddenly they heard a man laugh. It was an eerie sound that stopped them cold. They whirled around. At the bottom of the stairs, grinning up at them, was a man in overalls. His wiry hair stuck out from his head at odd angles. He wore a faded checked shirt under the overalls and he looked up at them, laughing quietly.

"So you want to talk to me, do you?" he said.

"Are you Ted?" Carol asked.

"That's me. Been caretaker around here longer than some folks can remember."

Slowly Carol and Charles walked down the stairs. They stopped near the caretaker, who continued to grin at them.

"We thought we just saw you go upstairs," Charles said. "That's where we were going."

The caretaker began chuckling. It was a low, strange kind of laugh. He laughed quietly, then shook his head. He lowered his face, as if embarrassed by his own smile, then peered upward at them. "Wasn't me," he said. "I've been on the other side. Mr. Benson found me and said you wanted to talk for a while."

"But then who—" Carol turned and half-pointed toward the top of the stairs.

"That was him," the caretaker said.

"Who?" Charles asked.

"*Him*," the caretaker said in a harsh whisper. "He's already been out in the graveyard. Now he's in here, going up the stairs as usual."

"I don't understand," said Carol.

"Was it cold awhile ago?" the caretaker suddenly asked. He watched their faces carefully, as if expecting to catch them in a lie.

"Yes," Carol said.

"Hey, that's right!" cried Charles. "It's not cold now!"

The caretaker chuckled again and shook his head. "Then it was him, all right. Probably still trying to stay away from the others."

"What others?" Carol asked. She looked quickly at Charles and felt goose bumps spread across her arms.

"Oh, you never see them," the caretaker said in a matter-of-fact tone. "All you do is hear them. They walk fast in their leather boots. Noisy, too. Can't get any sleep on some nights. Not around here. They walk up and down the halls, making all that sound. You don't ever see anybody, but they're looking for him, just the same. And all he does is go up and down this staircase and fool around out there in the graveyard. Plumb silly," the caretaker said, "him sitting out there with his lantern."

"Does Mr. Benson know about all this?" Carol asked. Charles looked at her and saw she had been scribbling notes while the caretaker was talking.

"He knows all right," the caretaker said. He laughed once, a short snorting sound. "But he pretends they're not here. Just goes on about his business. Those steps fool him sometimes, though." The caretaker laughed.

"Are you trying to tell us there are ghosts up here?" Charles asked.

"You felt the cold, didn't you?"

"Yes, sir."

"You saw him going up these stairs, didn't you?"

"Yes, sir."

"You hear the footsteps?"

"Yes, sir."

"All right then." The caretaker watched them,

grinning. Then he said, "I have to get back to work. I don't have time to stand around here. But I thank you for wanting to talk to me."

He turned abruptly and walked rapidly down the corridor until they could no longer see him.

Carol and Charles just stood still for a moment. They looked at each other. "I think we have enough inside information," Charles said after a moment.

"Yes," Carol agreed quickly. "We'd better go back to the office."

CHAPTER 5

Nearly running, they left the stairs and hurried up the corridor, hoping to catch up with the caretaker. But by the time they circled the corner, the man was no longer in sight.

"It's as if he disappeared," Carol said.

That was when the lights went out.

"Come on!" Charles told her. He took her by the hand and walked rapidly down the long, deserted hallway. "The office should be this way," he said. But when they turned another corner they saw nothing but darkness.

"This isn't right," Carol said. "Maybe we should have turned the other way."

Together, they retraced their steps, found the stairs again, and started out in a different direction. Gradually they both realized they were lost.

"What are we going to do?" Carol asked.

"Don't worry. We'll find the office."

They continued slowly along in the dark. They had nearly reached another turnoff when they heard the footsteps again. "Listen!" Carol whispered. They stopped, still holding hands. The rapid footsteps were coming from behind them.

"They're coming this way!" Carol cried.

"Hurry!" Charles told her. He pulled her against the wall. They stood there, waiting in the darkened shadows. The footsteps grew louder, seemed to be growing closer.

"We'll have to make a run for it!" Charles whispered.

Together they darted blindly down the corridor. Their own footsteps drowned out the others. They stopped for a moment, listening. But the footsteps were still there, following them, trying to catch up.

"Oh, Charles! What are we going to do?"

"Keep running. The office has to be this way!"

Without waiting for her to speak, Charles ran again, pulling Carol along behind him. They rushed through the darkness, then suddenly came to a halt. It was now too dark to see anything.

They had to stop running. They stood, backs once more pressed against the wall, and waited. The footsteps had slowed up now. They were coming at a slower pace. At the corner, the footsteps stopped, paused for a moment, then continued toward them.

Suddenly, in the dimness, they saw two figures. They moved silently, noiselessly except for the clack of the leather heels against the floor.

"They've found us!" Carol whispered.

"Be quiet!" Charles told her. They waited, breathing hard, watching the figures move silently toward them.

Without warning a beam of light cut through the darkness, licking along one wall. Carol screamed. It came before she could stop it. They were about to run again when the light hit them full in the face. Then a man said, "There you are! Thank goodness."

"Oh, Mr. Benson!" cried Carol. She ran toward him quickly, already smiling with relief. Behind Mr. Benson stood her father, his white hair shining through the darkness like a halo. "We didn't mean to frighten you," Mr. Benson said.

"You did a good job of it," Charles said.

"We thought you were ghosts," said Carol. All of them laughed.

"The lights probably went out because of the storm," Mr. Benson told them. "We were afraid you'd get lost."

"I've never been so happy to see anyone in my life!" Charles said.

Together they walked back through all the twists and turns of the corridor, Mr. Benson leading the way with his flashlight. As they passed the staircase again, a light came on in a nearby hallway.

"I guess Ted replaced the fuse," Mr. Benson said.

Soon they were inside the lighted office. "Have you finished with your interview?" Carol's father asked. Carol and Charles glanced at each other.

"Yes, sir. I think we've seen enough for one night."

"Then we'd better get going," Mr. Marshall said. "I'm afraid the rain is going to get worse."

They said good night to Mr. Benson and walked outside onto the porch. Luckily, the rain had slowed to a drizzle. Carol and Charles waited

while her father brought the car around to the steps.

As they ran down to the car, they turned once more and looked toward the graveyard. They saw the lantern moving among the tombstones.

"That caretaker should go inside," Carol told Charles. "You'd think he'd get pneumonia out in this weather."

"Well, as Mr. Benson said, he is a peculiar man."

"I suppose so," said Carol.

They opened the car door. Carol got in beside her father and Charles followed. At the same time both of them looked toward the huge front door of the museum. The caretaker stood there watching them. He didn't make a move. Then suddenly he grinned slightly to himself and carefully closed the door.

Charles and Carol looked back quickly toward the graveyard. It was dark now. There was no light.

And no one had seen it but the two of them and the caretaker.